CONTENTS

CHAPTER ONE

"I'll go in by myself," Scott said to his mum. "I *want* to go in by myself!"

He looked at all the other kids going in the gates. "I don't want them to think I'm a scaredy cat."

"If you're sure," said Mum.

Scott waved and smiled as his mum drove away. Then he turned around to look at his new school.

The playground
was nearly empty now.
He heard a bell and knew
he should run in
quickly, but his
legs felt weak
and shaky.

Scott's new
school was tall – very
tall. It was dark – very dark.
Everything about it was very
strange, very different and very,
very BIG!

All around the school there were high railings. It looked like a cage made to keep in some huge beast.

In the basement, Scott could see two grimy windows. The windows had bars across them.

Was something being kept down there? he wondered.

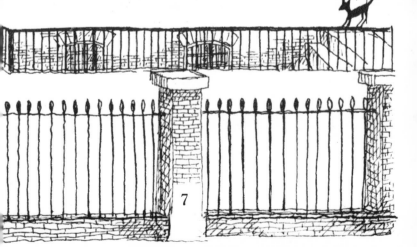

At his old house, Scott had gone to the school on the corner of his street. His old school was a small school. It had grass and trees all around it, and Scott had been happy there. He had lots of really good friends.

He didn't know anybody at this new place. Not one single person.

Scott took a deep breath, went through the gates, and across the playground. All he could hear was the sound of his own footsteps. He felt a bit sick.

Scott pushed the door into the school and stepped inside. It was quiet – very quiet. He peered into the office.

The secretary was busy talking on the phone. She didn't see him. In the distance, he could hear strange music and chanting.

I'm just late. They've started going into assembly, he told himself, but he couldn't help shivering.

Would he get in trouble for being late? Late on his very first day!

11

I'll just go to my classroom. I'm sure I can remember the way, he told himself.

The head teacher had showed Scott and his mum all around the school only a week ago.

Scott set off...

Five minutes later, he was lost.

There were so many corridors! So many stairs! He was now in a dark corridor. It was long and empty. It looked deserted, and it smelt dusty and strange.

Scott had not seen this part of the school on his visit. Was this part of the school kept a secret?

Slowly, he walked to the very end of the corridor. There, tucked into the corner, were some concrete stairs. These stairs led downwards.

Scott peered down the dark stairs. There were big, black footprints leading to a closed door. On the door there was a sign:

CHAPTER TWO

It was then that Scott noticed the
smell. It was a smell of heat and dust
and burning. It was a very strange
smell, and it was
coming from
behind the door
at the bottom
of the stairs.

What could be down there?

Scott could feel heat rising.
He could see light coming through
the cracks around the door.

Suddenly there was
a *flash* and a *roar*.

Scott jumped.

There was something in the
basement! And it was something
nasty… something monstrous…

What should I do? What should I do? he worried.

And then there was another **FLASH!** and a **BANG!** and a **RRRRrrrooaarr!**

Scott didn't stop to think. He ran.

He ran and ran and ran.
Up stairs …

… along corridors …

... round corners.

His heart was thumping hard
in his chest. He scrambled round
another corner and then he saw
where he was.

He was outside his classroom.
He knew it by the name on the
door and the display of dragon
paintings on the walls.

Mrs Archer, his new teacher,
had pointed it out last week when
he was visiting the school.

"We all did a fantastic project on dragons," she had said. "Everybody in this school is a dragon expert!"

Suddenly Scott knew the truth. There really *was* something in the basement. And that 'something' was a dragon.

There was a dragon coiled up and breathing fire deep below his new school!

CHAPTER THREE

Scott crept into the classroom.

"Sorry I'm late…" he muttered.

But Mrs Archer was busy, opening windows. She just waved at him to sit down at the front table.

"Don't worry. I'll sort you out in a minute," she said.

There were three other children on Scott's table. The red-haired boy next to him smiled and whispered his name.

"I'm Damon," he said.

The others just nodded and got on with their work.

The classroom was very quiet.
The only sound was a strange,
distant gurgling and glugging.
And it was so *hot*.

Everyone had taken off their
jumpers. Some were trying to fan
themselves with exercise books,
but no one was complaining.

It was so hot that Scott could hardly breathe. He looked around.

Why wasn't anybody saying anything? he wondered.

Why was everybody just getting on with their work as if it was normal to be boiled alive in a classroom?

And what was that noise?

The gurgling and glugging seemed to be getting louder and louder. And closer and closer?

Scott couldn't stand it any longer. He had a terrible feeling that something awful was going to happen. Shyly, he put up his hand.

"Please, Miss," he said. "It's boiling hot … and there's a strange noise…"

"Oh that!" said Mrs Archer.
"It's just Stovie up to his tricks
again. We'll have to get
Mr Crawley to sort
it out. He's the
only one who can
control the beast."

"Shall I go
to the basement
and find him?"
said Damon, the
red-haired boy.

"NO!" snapped the teacher.
"I've told you before. No one is
to go to the basement. EVER.
It's very dangerous. Is that clear?"

Everyone nodded.
Someone sighed. Mrs Archer
opened another window.

And then a
strange man came
into the room.

The man was
tall and very
hairy. He had
a thick beard,
long hair and
bushy eyebrows.
He was the
hairiest man
Scott had
ever seen.

There was even hair sprouting out of his ears and nose.

But the strangest thing was that he was covered in black streaks and soot. His hands and fingernails were dirty, and a smell of burning surrounded him.

Is that the dragon keeper? Scott wondered.

"Who's that?" whispered Scott.

"It's Creepy Crawley!" said Damon. "He's the one who looks after Stovie. Don't get on the wrong side of him!"

Mr Crawley spoke to Mrs Archer. "I'm sorry," he said. "The beast isn't behaving today. I may have overfed it. We're all going to roast!"

Soon it was playtime. Scott didn't like the idea of going into the playground with a lot of children he had never met before. And he couldn't stop thinking about the thing in the basement. It was all so strange, he was beginning to think he had imagined it.

He took a deep breath and decided: he would try to find those steps. He would try to find the dragon.

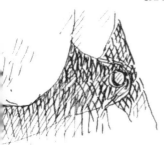

CHAPTER FOUR

Scott set off to find the basement steps again. It wasn't easy, and he was worried in case he met a teacher and had to explain where he was going. He didn't want to have to explain. He didn't want to

get into trouble. He was just about to give up – then he saw the steps.

Don't be scared, he said to himself. *Just go up to the door and peep through the crack.*

He followed the trail of sooty marks... down one stair... then two... then three.

He tried not to be scared of the smells. He tried not to be scared by the gurgling and glugging sounds coming through the door. He tried not to be scared of the shadows. But then he heard the sound of footsteps and the door at the bottom of the stairs opened...

It was the hairy
man. Creepy Crawley.
The dragon keeper!

DANGER!
DO
NOT
ENTER

"What are you doing!" roared Mr Crawley. "No children are allowed here! I'm going to take you straight to see the head!"

And that's what he did.

Soon a shaking Scott was standing in front of Mrs Witchley, the head teacher.

"What's all this about then?" she asked.

"I ...I ...was trying to see the thing in the basement," Scott stuttered. "I've heard it roaring. I've felt its heat. I know you've got a dragon down there!"

Mrs Witchley shook her head. "He knows you're keeping a dragon, Mr Crawley," she sighed. Then she looked at Scott and said: "I think it's time we introduced you to Stovie. Take him down to the basement, Mr Crawley!"

As they marched back down the maze of long, dark corridors, Scott's mind was bubbling with thoughts and fears:

Why are they taking me back to the basement?

What are they going to do?

Are they going to feed me to the **dragon**?

37

At the bottom of the concrete steps, Mr Crawley swung the door open. Mrs Witchley stood well back. There was a terrible wave of heat and sound.

"Scott, meet Stovie," said Mr Crawley.

Scott had never seen anything like it. It was huge. It was noisy. It was covered in soot...

But it wasn't a dragon.

CHAPTER FIVE

"Stovie is our old boiler," Mrs Witchley explained. "It heats the school. That's *heats* not *eats* the school! Sometimes it makes it a bit too hot – like today," she smiled.

"Oh..." Scott's voice sounded very small. He knew his face was going pink – and it wasn't just because of the heat.

"Only Mr Crawley knows how to control the old thing," explained Mrs Witchley. "We always say Stovie's a bit of a beast – but I never thought of calling it a dragon before!"

Scott's face was now bright
red – except for the places where
it was streaked with soot. He
came up the basement stairs
slowly, one step, two steps.
Behind him came Mrs
Witchley and
Mr Crawley.

Mrs Witchley brushed soot and cobwebs from her hair. "We don't allow children to come down here. The place is too hot and dirty. It just isn't safe."

Scott kept his eyes fixed on his feet. He had never felt so silly in all his life.

There was no dragon.

There was no mystery.

There was just a big, dark school where he didn't have any friends. He sighed. Life couldn't get any worse. Then he looked up...

Damon and Madison and Mia, the two girls from his table, were coming along the corridor and they were all pointing at him.

Oh no! thought Scott. *Now everyone's going to make fun of me.*

"There you are!" said Damon. "We've been looking everywhere for you. Do you want to play with us?"

"You're all covered in soot!" said Madison. "What happened?"

So Scott told them.

"What an adventure!" said Damon. "I wish *I* could solve a mystery."

Scott smiled. He was feeling much better now. He had some new friends. No one was making fun of him – and he wasn't afraid of a dragon any more.

They all went out into the playground and Scott pointed out the basement window. "I can't believe I thought there was a dragon living down there!" he laughed.

It was then that they heard the growl, a long, deep growl. The new friends looked at each other. Perhaps there *was* a thing in the basement, after all! Maybe they could solve the mystery together.

9781472967558

Look out for more books in the
BLOOMSBURY READERS SERIES

There are signs of a ghost in Grandpa's creaky old house and strange noises at night. So when Adam dares his brother and sister to hunt down the ghost in the graveyard at midnight, who will be brave enough?